D1489609

Joanne Oppenheim

James Will Never Die

ROCKLAND PUBLIC LIBRARY ROCKLAND MAINE

Illustrated by True Kelley

Dodd, Mead & Company ☆ New York

Text copyright © 1982 by Joanne Oppenheim · Illustrations copyright © 1982 by True Kelley
All rights reserved · No part of this book may be reproduced in any form without
permission in writing from the publisher · Printed in the United States of America

1   2   3   4   5   6   7   8   9   10

Library of Congress Cataloging in Publication Data

Oppenheim, Joanne.
  James will never die.

Summary: In their pretend games, an older brother always seems to come out on top.
[1. Brothers and sisters — Fiction. 2. Play — Fiction] I. Kelley, True, ill. II. Title
        PZ7.O616Jam   1982   [E]   82-45374
        ISBN 0-396-08067-7   AACR2

*This is for my sons
and for my mother, who often said,
"Don't worry, they're just playing."*
— *J.O.*

*To my brother, Mark Kelley III,
master of the dramatic death scene.*
— *T.K.*

"Tony! Hey, Tony! Where are you?"

That's my brother, James, calling me. He wants me to play. But I'm not playing his games anymore because James isn't fair. No matter what we play, James will never die.

Like yesterday, we were playing Wagon Train. It was James and Bobby against Kenny and me. We were crossing the Rocky Mountains and winter was coming. The wind howled and dust blinded our eyes.

"We'll make camp in the canyon," I said. I was boss of the wagon train. We were deep in Cheyenne country. We knew they were out there, ready to stop any settlers crossing their sacred hunting grounds. I built a fire and stood watch.

Suddenly drums echoed through the canyon and
James came racing on his horse, swinging his hatchet
and screaming his terrible war cry.

"Ant-ta-na-na-nee-nee!"

I aimed straight at him. POW! POW! I got him.

But James yelled, "You missed!" Then he grabbed
me, and Bobby sneaked up on Kenny.

"No fair!" I told James. "I got you, ask Kenny."
But James only said, "Quay, quay, Kanish-a-na-bee"
to Bobby. They pretended they didn't speak English.
James is always pretending.

Once James said we would go on an expedition together, digging for dinosaur bones. The sun was blazing hot and our throats were dry, but we kept digging. Suddenly my shovel hit something hard.

"Bones!" I hollered.

Bobby and Kenny came running.

"Look at this!" yelled Kenny.

"They're gigantic!" shouted Bobby.

"James!" I hollered. "It's a brontosaurus!"

"No way," James called from across the field. "Brontosauruses lived near the water. There's no water around here."

"A long time ago there was," I answered.

But James didn't pay any attention. Instead he called, "Holy cow! Come on over here and get a load of this! Hurry!"

Bobby and Kenny ran over. I walked.

"I'm telling you guys, this is it," James said. "A stegosaurus egg, for sure."

"Says who?" I asked.

But Bobby agreed with James. "Yup. It's an egg all right."

"I know," said James. "Come on, help me dig it up."

How come James always thinks he knows everything?

Another time we were playing Outer Space. I was
from the distant planet Anton, soaring through deep
darkness searching for an E.S.S., an Enemy Space Ship.
It was a dangerous mission, but I was fearless. I had
my scanner beams open, listening.

ping ping ping

I heard it faintly.

Ping Ping Ping

The sound grew louder.

PING PING PING

I switched on my magnetic field to pull it into range. Now I had it in my sights.

PING PING PING PING PING PING

Quickly I fired my micromatic cannon. Vroom!

PING PING PING

I fired two more times. Vroom! Vroom! "Direct hit!" I called. "Disintegrate!"

"POONG! POONG! This is Enemy Space Ship J-A-M-E-S. My force field is fixed. POONG! Your fire can't get through. POONG! Too bad, Antonite. My force field is bouncing back your fire. POONG! POONG! You're doomed, Antonite."

After that I told James I was sick of his tricks. James said, "It's only a game, Tony. Don't take it so hard."

Then this morning he promised we'd have a great time. We were climbing Mount Everest, just James and me. He said I could put the flag up.

The wind was burning cold and our hands and feet were numb. "Watch your step," I called. "That's sheer ice."

"We're almost there, Tony," said James. "I can see the top. What a sight!"

"We made it, James. We made it," I said.

I was about to put the flag up when James yelled, "Oh, no, Tony! Avalanche! WATCH OUT BELOW! Your rope, Tony! Your rope is fraying. Here, fast, catch hold of my hand. Oh, no. Too late. Oh, no, my only brother. Gone, gone, gone! I'll never forget you, Tony. Farewell!"

How come James can live through an avalanche, enemy fire, and everything else? Somehow I had to get even with him.

"Tony! Tony!"

That's James. He's still looking for me.

"Tony! Hey, Tony! Come out, come out wherever you are. Kenny and Bobby are here. Come on, let's play."

"Okay, James," I called. "Look, I found a treasure map. Let's play pirates."

"Ay-ay!" James saluted. "I'll be the captain."

I knew James would say that. Now I had him where
I wanted him. He had fallen into my trap.

We set sail with the tide. It was smooth sailing until
nightfall. Then a terrible gale began whipping up the
waves. They were as tall as mountains.

"Courage, Mates," James ordered. "Keep a sharp lookout."

"Danger off the starboard bow," I called.

"What is it?" Bobby cried. "I can't make it out."

"A reef!" I shouted. "A coral reef!"

"It will rip us apart!" screamed Kenny.

"Steady, Mates. I'll pull us through," James boasted.

"Too late!" I hollered. "It's dead ahead!"

In seconds our ship was smashed from stem to stern
and sinking fast.

"Abandon ship! Abandon ship!" James ordered.

"Man the lifeboats!" I shouted, grabbing Kenny and
pulling him in with me. Bobby jumped in after us.

"Wait for me!" James called. "Wait for me!"

"Shove off, Mates!" I yelled. "He'll have to go down with his ship. The captain *always* goes down with his ship. Too bad, James!"

I did it. It felt so good. I was finally even with James.

"He's down in Davy Jones's locker," said Kenny.

"Just keep rowing," said Bobby, "and don't look back."

So, there we were, tossing on the open sea in our lifeboat, wondering if and when we'd ever see land again. Our pirate ship was gone and so was James. Only for some reason, as I looked out on the stormy sea, I started feeling a little sorry about James. Then I spotted something off in the distance.

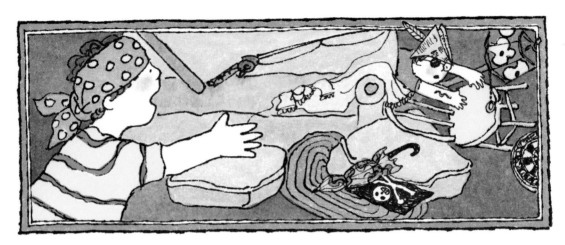

At first all I could see was a piece of the mast floating with the wreckage on the waves. Then I spotted him hanging on, more dead than alive.

"Captain!" I shouted.

"H-e-l-p!"

His voice was so weak we could hardly hear him. He was losing his grip. In another minute he'd be a goner.

"Sharks!" Kenny hollered. "They're trailing him!"

"He's done for!" shouted Bobby.

I put my knife between my teeth and dove into the raging sea.

"Put him out of his misery," called Bobby.

I could have let him drown or let the sharks finish him off...

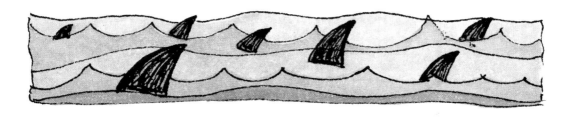

...but I didn't. I saved him, and I wasn't sorry. It was worth it to hear him say, "Tony, I owe you my life."

"Land ho!" I shouted. "Land ho!"